THREAT!

A story of Mary Slessor

by

Karen Doherty

rooshie doo

Published by Gallus Publications,
PO Box 29055,
Dunfermline KY11 4YL

Cover design by Liam Doherty, with original artwork by Cameron Renwick (front cover) and Hannah Lynn (back cover), both of Commercial Primary School, Dunfermline. Illustrations by Frank McCormick.

The right of Karen Doherty to be identified as the author of this work has been asserted in accordance with the Copyright, Designs and Patents Act 1988.

ISBN 0-9546625-3-9

A catalogue record for this book is available from the British Library.

Printed and bound by Printing Services (Scotland) Ltd., Broomhead Drive, Dunfermline.

Author's acknowledgements

I would like to thank the staff of Dundee Central Library for help in researching this book; and also to acknowledge the work of Elizabeth Robertson in her book 'Mary Slessor'.

This book is dedicated to my mother, another wee wifie who grips on well.

Karen Doherty, Kirkcaldy July 2004

DUNDEE

CHAPTER ONE

Eleven year olds Mary Slessor and Elspeth Grant could feel many eyes upon them as they walked. A familiar voice sneered behind them.

'Quine? What's a quine Mary? Sounds like swine tae me? Is a quine a swine Mary? You'd ken the best.'

'Haud your tongue, ye dirty midden. Does your mither ken you speak like that? You ken fine whit I said.' Mary whirled round, scarlet with temper.

'Go on, tell us - tell us aboot the swines in Aberdeen. Does a'body cry the lassies swines or is it jist you?'

'Shut up or I swear I'll swing for you.' muttered Mary, glaring at her. Elspeth tugged her sleeve.

'Ignore her Mary, she cannae help being donnert.'

Mary glanced at her friend Elspeth and knew she was right but Mary still hated Katie Murray. Ever since Mary had arrived in Dundee Katie had made her life miserable, teasing her about her accent. So what if she sounded a bit different? She was from Aberdeen, not the moon! Elspeth had been her first friend when she moved

1

to Dundee and she was her best friend now.

Katie and the other girls had followed Mary and Elspeth from school, over the cobbles and into the mill.

The taunting continued all the way.

They made their way into the cloakroom to hang up their shawls and get ready for their shift. Mary didn't mind being a halftimer but she hated being on the same shift as

Katie Murray. Still, she had no choice - working at the mill paid the rentman.

Mary glowered at Katie across the room but took her apron from the hook and bent down to redo her bootlaces which had come undone.

'Haw Elspeth!' Katie smirked, tying her long apron straps behind her. 'Mind ye dinnae coup the stack like last week. Auld Mathieson'll hae yer guts for garters. Pick up yer besom and sweep up the stoor like a guid wee lassie. It's a' yer guid for. Blind as a bat and twice as ugly.'

Elspeth cringed but said nothing, hanging her shawl on the hook. She was mortified. Everyone knew Katie was talking about Elspeth's squint. Elspeth kept her back to Katie but knew every girl in the room was waiting for her reaction. She decided to make a joke of it.

'Ah but ye see I'm aye on the look for a handsome husband. Lookin' baith weys at the same time is a lot quicker.'

There was a nervous giggle among the other girls. But Mary wasn't going to let her friend by insulted. 'You take that back Katie Murray,' she said, hands on hips.

'Ha! I might have kent you pair wid stick the gither,' laughed Katie, 'Ugly Elspeth and Mary the swine! A fine pair.'

'I said take that back!' said Mary, her eyes ablaze.

'Mary, jist leave it...' whispered Elspeth.

Katie looked at Mary long and hard. Mary was smaller and lighter than her. She was no threat.

'I'll no' tak it back and you cannae mak me.'

'Can I no'!' roared Mary, hurling herself at the unsuspecting Katie. She knocked her backwards onto the benches and it took Katie a moment to recover. She angrily brushed hair from her face and charged straight back at Mary, arms flailing in rage. Mary, being smaller and more nimble jumped aside causing Katie to crash into Mr. Mathieson, the gaffer, who'd come to investigate the

commotion. He was not a man to cross. He had been known to whip slow workers with some leftover jute if the mood took him. Everybody was afraid of him.

'Oomphhh! Whit the divil...? Murray! Again! ...' he spluttered, picking himself up off the floor and rubbing his ribs.

'I...I...I'm sorry, Mr. Mathieson, it was an accident...' beseeched Katie, scrambling to her feet.

'Nae mair! You're aye causing bother Murray. Get your belongings an' get doon tae the office. You're gettin'your books the day.'

'Aw please Mr. Mathieson, dinnae say that...' Katie said, clutching at his waistcoat as he walked away.

'She did it! It was that Mary Slessor. She ca'ed me ower.'

'What? That wee smout? She couldnae ca' ower a *speug*. So you're a liar tae, Murray?' He brushed her off angrily but she followed him in desperation, gabbling as she walked.

None of the other girls said a word for they were not fond of Katie Murray and they all silently hoped that they'd seen the last of her. Mary knew it was wrong to enjoy the misfortune of others but she couldn't help smiling. Elspeth paused in the doorway and checked around the corner before throwing herself onto her knees and pleading with her broom. Her voice became the voice of Katie.

'She did it, Mr Mathieson! It was Mary Slessor, Mr Mathieson! Three bags full, Mr Mathieson! Can I lick your boots Mr Mathieson?'

All the girls clapped their hands and laughed out loud. Elspeth was always good fun.

'Does this mean I can gie the besom up an' get promoted tae Tea Jenny?' Still smiling the girls headed off together to start their shift, chattering and joking. Maybe this was going to be a good day after all.

CHAPTER TWO

Sixteen years later Mary and Elspeth were still best friends. Elspeth now worked at the local bakery and Mary was fulltime at the mill but they still saw each other most days.

It was time to go home. The two girls shuddered in the cold air, drawing their shawls tightly around their heads and huddling close against the bitter wind.

'How's your Mother's cough been Elspeth? Mary asked, eyes on her boots.

'Ach, no' sae good, Mary. That last poultice didnae mak much difference. I'm feart fur her. Maybe the Parish could gie her some liniment? Or a tonic?' Elspeth sighed and wiped her nose on her sleeve.

'Try not to vex yourself.' said Mary, making a mental note to ask her mother to call in. The two girls walked on in silence, deep in thought. Suddenly, Elspeth changed the subject.

'So are you sure ye want tae be a missionary ? An' are you still mad keen on that Livingstone fella?'

'If you mean Mr David Livingstone, ye cheeky besom, then aye...' laughed Mary.

'Ye ken fine who I mean. I jist dinnae see the appeal masel'. Every time I see ye, ye hae your nose in a book aboot Africa.'

'Oh Elspeth. Think whit it'd be like tae travel the world. Meet new folk, see new places...If I could be jist a wee bit like him...' Mary's eyes sparkled as she spoke. 'I cannae wait tae start my training in Edinburgh.'

'Well I made ye this, so's ye can wave cheerio tae me an' dicht yer een.' She handed Mary a small embroidered handkerchief. Mary stopped walking and stared at it. The stitching was not neat and Mary wasn't sure if it had a flower or a heart on it but she thought it was beautiful. Mary vowed always to keep in touch with her dearest friend.

Later that night Mary was walking alone through the dark, cobbled streets of the city chappin' doors, Bible firmly clasped in her hand. Sometimes folk would welcome her in, sometimes folk laughed at her and sometimes they slammed the door in her face. Mary didn't mind, she took it all in her stride.

Turning the corner into a shadowy alleyway, Mary could make out three teenagers leaning against a wall, one sitting on the steps of a close and one sitting on a low dyke swinging something on a rope. They were all drinking. Mary took a deep breath and approached them cheerfully.

'Wid you laddies be interested in coming tae a service

in the Quarry Pend, in Queen Street this Sunday?

'The Kirk? Hah! There's nuthin' there for us,' scoffed one, spitting pointedly on the ground beside her. Mary's eyes narrowed but she stood her ground. 'How do ye ken? Hiv ye ever been?'

The teenager swinging the rope walked closer. In the gaslight she could see that on the end of the rope was a piece of metal that looked as if it might have been an old padlock. It was clearly big and heavy because the swing was slow but tight. As he approached, the metal got closer and closer to Mary. The teenager did not take his eyes off Mary and she didn't take her eyes off him. He was clearly the leader of the gang. He steadily and deliberately swung the padlock in a slow circle, closer and closer to Mary's face.

'A wee lassie like you shidnae be hingin' aboot the streets at nicht.'

'Fit an' able laddies like you shidnae be hingin' aboot drinkin'.' Mary replied, folding her arms.

The swinging weight was now so close its draught fluttered tiny wisps of hair above her ear. Still, she didn't flinch. Her eyes were fixed upon his. The weight was swinging faster and stronger as the seconds passed. Eventually it began to brush against her forehead but Mary didn't move. Her heart was pounding but she felt strangely calm. The weight was so close she could smell it. The gang stood silently watching. The youth swinging the rope licked his lips nervously. Mary took a deep breath and challenged him.

'So. What'll it be? Will ye come on Sunday or are ye too feart? Ye can birl that thing a' day, it'll mak nae difference. I'm no' budgin' till ye say ye'll come.' The gangleader laughed and dropped the weight. 'She's game boys!' he admitted and stepped towards her. He felt a little ashamed as he took her hand.

'Aye we'll be there. Whit aboot it lads?' He looked at Mary. 'Nae hard feelins then?'

Mary grinned, nodding, and set about telling them all about the fun they would have on church trips to the country. Mary decided not to tell them just yet of her passion for hitching up her skirts and climbing to the tops of trees. Maybe they'd all had enough excitement for one evening!

They walked back down through the alley together and Mary couldn't help thinking that tonight was a special night. What had seemed so dangerous a moment ago, now seemed like a faraway dream. She watched the teenagers

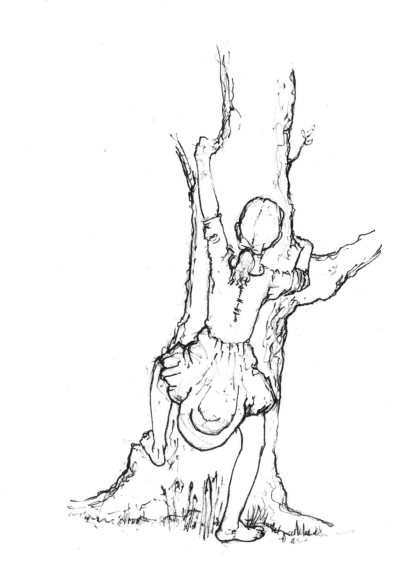

amble down the alley towards the Cowgate. They were noisy and boisterous - relieved that the tension had been broken. They weren't bad, they were just bored. She suspected that with a little nudge in the right direction life could change for them, in a very good way. Mary was certain about one thing – missionary work was what she wanted to do. Dundee was a great starting point but she wondered what might lie ahead if she travelled to Africa like her hero, David Livingstone. Once she was in Edinburgh a whole new adventure would begin for her. Mary just couldn't wait.

CHAPTER THREE

Two months later Mary found herself thinking about that night in the alleyway, the gangleader and how he had really turned his life around. Her life had changed too - in so many ways.

She was now more than halfway through her training at Moray House and had already learned so much. It hadn't been easy though. Things were very different here. Life was different, people were different, and Mary herself was different. She had been learning what to expect when she arrived in Africa. The most difficult part was learning how to become an 'agent'. Every day, she was reminded how ladies sent to do missionary work had to set the very best example and maintain the very highest standards of behaviour. She would be an 'agent' first and then become a missionary only when she earned that title. There had been times that Mary had doubted she would ever become the sort of 'lady' she was expected to be. It seemed that ladies simply never did the things she liked to do – climb, run, jump, sing, shout, laugh.

Worst of all were the lessons in elocution. Mary struggled to speak as the other trainees spoke, many from wealthy families. Some days it was just like being eleven again. Nonetheless, Mary loved the opportunity to read and study. When she read, she dreamed and when she dreamed, she dreamed of Africa. She smiled to herself – even the name sounded wonderful. *Calabar*.

'Mary! For the third time, please pay attention!'

Mary jumped with fright. Her book slipped to the floor and landed with a thud at her feet. Quiet giggles rippled round the library. Mary flushed and picked up the book, watched by the eagle-eyed tutor.

'Now, ladies, one quick reminder before we finish…the essays are to be returned to me by Friday. No later. Your training ends in two weeks, I do hope you will ALL make the most of this precious time to prepare effectively for your departure.' The tutor raised her eyebrows meaningfully at Mary who blushed a second time.

Gathering all her books, Mary went straight to her dorm to write to Elspeth. She longed to tell Elspeth of the wonderful news. She'd been told shortly after breakfast and every minute spent in studies had been torture. It had been all she could think about. In two weeks time she would be on her way!

Mary tossed her books onto the bed then sat at her desk to write. She chewed the end of her pen.

21 July 1876
Edinburgh

Dear Elspeth
Guess what! The news came today. The Foreign Mission Board has confirmed that I am to go to Calabar in West Africa! Isn't that wonderful news? It's like a dream come true. It certainly makes up for all the boring things we've done during training. I can't for the life of me work out why we need to know Latin - or the art of napkin folding! Your wee hanky will do me fine.

Anyway, like I say, I'll be heading off in two weeks time. Will you come to see me leave? Can you take the time off? We'll be sailing with the tide on the 5th of August. The ship is called the SS Ethiopia. Even the name excites me! Please say you'll come. I've already written to my mother and sisters, perhaps you could come with them? I'll write with more details later – I've got to go change for dinner.

Dinner! I can hardly believe I'm saying that. It still feels funny, although I'm getting used to eating so late. And these people eat so much in one go! It could feed a family for a fortnight. A wee jam piece would do me, or a lump of treacle toffee! They're not so keen on ladies chewing toffee round here but I'll sneak some with me for the trip.

Anyway, must dash. Can't be late for dinner – we ladies can't do that!

Take care
Mary

Two weeks later, at the age of twenty eight, Mary boarded the SS Ethiopia and waved to Elspeth, her mother and sisters on the quayside. Although it was late summer, the sky above was dreich, grey and heavy. Mary didn't

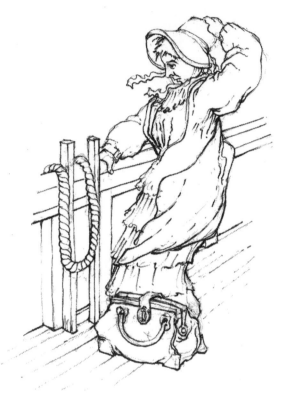

care. 15th August 1876 – she would remember this day always! The sails on the mast above her snapped and cracked in the wind, a wind that made her pale cheeks pink. Mary's stomach churned in excitement, and she hoped it was simply her nerves and not a bad omen.

Once more the wind lifted and Mary held on to her hat firmly. Her small, slim body struggled to stay still against the railing. Her mother was calling to her from below but Mary could not hear her above the hustle and bustle of the busy harbour. She shook her head and cupped her hand to her ear to indicate her problem and so her mother nodded and simply blew a kiss.

Even from that distance Mary knew her mother was weeping and her heart ached because of it. Seeing her sadness was almost too much to bear. It was a relief when the captain ordered the deckhands to cast off and raise the anchor. Mary breathed in deeply. This was it! She wiped her eyes and waved madly till they were tiny dots behind her. She was finally on her way.

CHAPTER FOUR

'Calabar! Calabar! All ashore for Calabar!'

Mary soaked up the sight of land like a thirsty child.

'Tread carefully ma'am, mind your step,' said a deckhand, grasping her elbow tightly as she edged her way along a makeshift bridge from the ship to the harbourside. Her long skirts hid the plank and she feared she might drop into the space between the ship and the pier. She barely had the strength to walk because the cursed seasickness had weakened her so. Had it really been only a month since she left Scotland? It had felt like an eternity. Mary hated being weak and even as she stumbled ashore she held her head high.

The smell of fish and sweat in the blistering heat was strong. The air was heavy and Mary found it hard to breathe. Her long, red hair was piled in a loose bun but it stuck to her head in limp strands about her face. She was hot, tired and tempted to be sick but her pride prevented her from doing so.

Wiping her forehead and neck with her handkerchief she allowed the deckhand to lead her to a ramshackle hut, facing the pier. Before she reached the door, it opened and a short, stout woman emerged dressed completely in black, her long skirts swishing heavily as she moved. She wore a crisp white lace collar pinned with a small cameo brooch. Her grey hair was firmly pinned beneath a stiff black hat, tied with a black ribbon.

'Good morning Miss Slessor, welcome to Calabar. My name is Mrs. Henshaw, I trust you are not too weary from your journey for we have yet some distance to go.' she said, indicating a small cart to the left of the hut.

Mary longed to lie down in a darkened room but knew there was little point in wasting time. She nodded weakly to Mrs. Henshaw and allowed herself to be helped, by the deckhand, onto the little wooden seat of the cart.

Gradually Mary became more aware of her surroundings. Watching the deckhand return to the ship she was struck by the number of black men and boys moving about the harbourside; loading supplies, unloading trade goods, carrying luggage and coiling ropes. Mary had lived all her life amongst fisherfolk but there was little resemblance here to Dundee or Aberdeen. Fishermen from home wore thick jumpers and heavy coats to protect them from the harsh North Sea. The water of the Tay was grey and dour to match the sky. Here though the sky was a brilliant blue and the water glittered with brightness. The surrounding area had a number of wooden buildings and storage depots for this was clearly a trading harbour. Each of the buildings was brightly coloured. Mary had never seen anything like it. Beyond the buildings lush vegetation erupted as far as the eye could see. The black men worked bare-backed and their skin shone in the sunlight. Mary averted her eyes and was surprised that she was feeling better despite the great heat and the movement of the cart.

Suddenly she realised that Mrs. Henshaw had been speaking to her,

'...and of course, there will be no question that you shall visit with me until you become accustomed to the ways of these poor unfortunates who need us so much.

You have much to learn, my dear, but rest assured you have friends aplenty to assist you.' Mary started to thank her but suddenly the cart struck a boulder on the muddy road. Both she and Mrs. Henshaw lurched suddenly to the left before the cart was righted by the driver.

'Gracious me! Francis! Are you mad? Don't be so clumsy! Our poor guest was nearly thrown to her death' she snapped, whacking the driver on the back of the head with her cane. Mary winced.

'I..I'm fine, Mrs. Henshaw, thank you. Just a wee bump in the road. The driver did well not to *coup* the cart.' blurted Mary.

Mrs. Henshaw looked at Mary in surprise, her displeasure clear. Her eyes narrowed to a glare.

'Miss Slessor, your graciousness does you credit but it is our Christian duty to correct the errors of our misguided

brothers and sisters. Once you have spent a little longer in Calabar you shall see that there are countless errors to attend.' She turned away to fix her eyes upon the horizon, fanning herself with a little ivory fan.

    Having travelled for a good hour through the lush grassland Mary learned that she had been fortunate with the weather that day. This was the middle of the rainy season and only the night before the road had been unpassable. Mary tried to concentrate on Mrs. Henshaw's words but her eyes and thoughts were drawn to the silent driver in front of them. The black curls on the back of his head were glistening with droplets of blood where the cane had left its mark. Mary bit her lip but said nothing. Her attention returned to Mrs. Henshaw who was telling her that she would be cared for by 'Mammy' and 'Daddy' Anderson and that there were many more friends at the mission station in Duke Town. There she would be expected to teach in the mission school and learn Efik, the local language. Mary could not wait. She was hot, exhausted and her boots felt like they were three sizes too small.

Eventually they arrived at their destination and Mary was greeted by her hosts and allowed to rest and freshen up before meeting Mrs. Henshaw's 'ladies'. In a flurry of gowns and handkerchiefs she was welcomed and invited to share any news from home. They sat together around a large table covered with a finely detailed lace tablecloth. A young servant girl, head bowed, moved silently between them with cool drinks and fresh fruit.

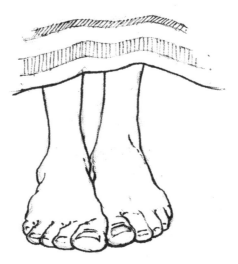

'Bella! Your feet are bare again. How dare you! Go at once into the house and put those boots and stockings on. Those ones from the mission box. Where is your decency?' snorted the stout lady at the far end of the table. This was clearly her house. Mary watched in uncomfortable silence as the startled girl nodded briefly and disappeared inside. 'Honestly! I don't know how many times I've told her. I know it's my Christian duty to educate these poor girls but one finds it so wearisome to repeat again and again.'

Mary cleared her throat and joked softly. 'It is gey hot out here so perhaps going barefoot isn't such a bad idea. In fact, I wouldn't mind releasing my toes from their trappings right now!' The older women looked at each other in horror, then one started to laugh. The others soon did the same.

'For a moment I thought you were serious Miss Slessor. Clearly we are out of touch with current humour from home. Barefoot, indeed.' Once again, there was a tinkle of laughter. Mary said nothing but noticed that the little servant girl was secretly watching them all through the window. She felt very uncomfortable.

The rest of the evening was spent seeing round the school and the infirmary. Everyone was very friendly towards her, but she felt a growing discomfort. Had she made a mistake in coming here? Was it really what she wanted or hoped it would be? Did she really want to become one of Mrs Henshaw's ladies? It was far too early to tell. She decided to write to Elspeth and her mother.

15th August 1876
Duke Town

Dearest Mother,
Although the journey was a trial, I thank God that I have arrived safely. The people here behave kindly towards me and I am learning a great deal. My lodgings are more than adequate. 'Mammy' and 'Daddy' Anderson have seen to my every need and Mrs. Henshaw ensures I am up to date with all the goings on. I believe I shall enjoy teaching the wee ones and tending the sick. I miss you already and trust that you are well. How are my darling sisters? I shall write more when I am not so weary. It has been a busy day! Please write soon, dearest mother. A word or two will do.

Your loving daughter
Mary

Mary folded the paper neatly and wrote the address on the back. She would find out in the morning how it could be delivered to the ship. Although she ached all over she was very excited to be finally at her destination and was desperate to share it with someone. She didn't think Mrs Henshaw would be very interested in her palaver. She picked up her pen and thought for a moment before continuing to write. She grinned to herself, imagining Elspeth's excitement and delight when she read her letter. Elspeth had made her promise to write often with all the details of her adventures. Mary knew that Elspeth would miss her and she gazed at the embroidered handkerchief

Elspeth had given her before she left. Taking a deep breath Mary set about writing her friend a letter to remember.

15ᵗʰ August 1876
Duke Town

Dearest Elspeth,
I hope this letter finds you well. I should have been glad of your company onboard ship. The SS Ethiopia is a fine vessel but I do not have sailor's legs. Your wit and good humour would have served as a welcome distraction to my sea sickness. Indeed

any wit would have been welcome. As it was I had only the ship's cat for company and even it left me after the first week!

The captain and crew had little time for a green passenger and I was left to my own devices for much of the journey. I should not think I shall be left to my own devices in Calabar however. Already I am informed that genteel ladies do not do the things I long to do. In fact, dear friend, a wicked thought came to me today as I worked, wilting in the heat. I saw a large knife upon a table. No, my wicked thoughts did not turn to murder! I simply longed to cut off this blessed hair which hangs from me like a heavy, winter curtain. Dare I do it my dear? In any case, sleep tugs at my eyes. I shall dream of being shaven headed, like a newly shorn sheep at market.

Write soon and tell me of home

With fondest regards

Mary.

Mary blew out the candle and got ready for bed. Whatever lay ahead for her would have to wait until morning. She uttered a quick prayer of thanks then laid down her head and went straight to sleep.

CHAPTER FIVE

It took Mary weeks to get used to the sound of thousands of insects and birds waking her in the morning. It was almost a roar in her head. She had been used to early rises and loud noises since her childhood days at the mill but this was so different.

Here her day was filled with prayer, teaching, nursing and talking with local people. She called these big talking sessions a palaver. She fell into bed each night tired but happy. She knew her help was needed and she loved working with the local people, who were far friendlier than the other female agents.

'Will you please wear your sun bonnet when you are out in company, Miss Slessor?'

Mary stopped digging and straightened her already

aching back. With a deep sigh she turned to face Mrs. Henshaw.

'As I've told you a dozen times before Mrs. Henshaw, I don't need the bonnet and I don't want to wear it. It makes my head itch terribly. It's hot enough with this dreadful weight of hair on my head. I just can't bear to work like that.'

'We all have our sacrifices to make Miss Slessor. Some of us manage to suffer in silence.'

'I doubt you could do anything in silence.' Mary muttered, chopping angrily at the ground with her hoe.

Mrs. Henshaw eyed her suspiciously but hadn't heard.

'I...that is...the ladies feel that you should keep your hair covered at all times, Miss Slessor.'

Mary had had enough. She threw down the hoe and marched across to a pile of tools. She picked up a knife and marched back to Mrs. Henshaw. The older woman was too surprised to be frightened.

'I won't wear a hat! And if the sight of my bare hair offends you that much then it will have to go...'

She undid her hair pins and let her red hair fall in a long ponytail. She grabbed it, looked Mrs Henshaw straight in the eye and hacked it off with the knife. She waved the ponytail at her, grinning triumphantly.

'Mad! You are completely mad!' screeched Mrs Henshaw, stumbling backwards. She gathered her skirts and hurried away to tell the others, declaring Mary a lunatic as she did so.

Mary returned the knife to the pile and started to laugh. She was tempted to nail the ponytail to a doorframe but tossed it aside instead.

She worked hard and for the next four years she
made the best of things; but her patience with her fellow
workers was wearing thin. Mary had long since stopped
wearing boots, preferring instead to go barefoot like the
villagers. Despite being encouraged in Edinburgh to
improve her speech and become more ladylike, Mary never
quite felt comfortable with the other female agents. Many
of them behaved as if they were still in Princes Street. Mary
however felt that Calabar was her home. She felt she
belonged. She felt at home amongst the people.

The letters to and from her other home in Dundee,
however, continued to sustain her.

1880
Duke Town

Dearest mother,

I hope this letter finds you well. I am sorry the paper is so poor but it is all the scrap I have. We are awaiting supplies from further down the coast. There is much unrest here. Bitter fighting in Lagos and beyond continues to create problems for us with regard to trade, and naturally the arrival of the mission boxes. Fear not Mother for I am safe and well. I have many friends amongst the villagers and am quite fluent in Efik, their native tongue. I found today that I am to be reassigned to Old Town which is three miles upriver. The trip should go well as the river is not swollen and the canoes are soundly built. In many ways I am looking forward to this new challenge.
Your loving daughter
Mary

Mary laid her pen down and looked up to find Mrs Henshaw watching her. Despite the heat Mary felt suddenly very cold.

'I wonder if I might have a word, Miss Slessor.'

'Of course, Mrs Henshaw. I was about to join the other women in a wee bit of basket weaving, will you join me?' said Mary, rising.

'Ah no, it's about the women actually.' said Mrs Henshaw, smoothing a seam on her tight black jacket and tugging at her crisp, white gloves. Mary stopped in the doorway and turned to face her.

'What about the women?'

'Well, I...the other agents feel that it is not appropriate for you to be associating yourself quite so freely with these…people.'

'I don't understand what you mean.' said Mary, folding her arms and glowering.

'You seem too… shall we say …familiar. You chatter on in their strange language instead of the Queen's good English. Our task is to teach, tend the sick and spread the Gospel. We are here to help these unfortunates, not to be their friends, you know.'

'Rubbish!' Mary was red with rage.

'How dare you!' snapped Mrs Henshaw, striding towards the door. 'Squatting in the sun has addled your brain.'

'Aye well, maybe so but at least I'm no' hirplin' aboot like a hoodie craw a' day.'

Mary had always been outspoken but even she was surprised by her words. Her mother might not have approved but Mary had no regrets.

Mrs Henshaw's eyes were as black as her skirt as she passed Mary, hissing, 'I don't know where the Mission Board dragged you from. You've never fitted in. The sooner you're out of here the better.'

Mary couldn't agree more. She'd rather face any dangerous tribes than another day with Mrs Henshaw and her ladies.

1880
Duke Town

Dear Elspeth

Thank you for your last letter which made me laugh so heartily my pupils feared I was weeping. I do indeed miss the plum pudding but hope that you shall send me some from the bakery and I shall eat it for breakfast, dinner, supper and breakfast again! There is nothing so fine as a sweet plum pudding. In the meantime I shall make do with my delicious cornmeal mush and yams. In truth it may be some time before I can have anything else for the trade routes are greatly troubled and we have no idea when things may change. In god we trust!

I was informed today that I am to be reassigned. I fear the good ladies of this parish have had enough of me. My bare feet and shorn head offend them so mortally that I am to be banished to the hinterland. I will not be sorry to go. I came to help those most in need and this I shall do, with god's help. I am to go to Old Town which is three miles up river. There are rumours that this shall be a formidable challenge but one I shall take up and gladly. My only concern is that in the valleys of that area, great mists rise up - and with them come great clouds of biting insects (worse than Scottish midges!) which lead to a dreadful fever from which many are left withered or dead. I cannot say I am unafraid but there are many who face worse.

I think Mrs. Henshaw and her cronies will be glad to see me go. Today she asked me once again to wear a hat and once more I declined saying there was little need. She nearly swallowed her fan. I think she and her friends had more than a little to do with my transfer but no matter. I shall make the best of it and see what befalls me. I think she would suffer a faint if she knew what the villagers said about her, in her presence. (She has never troubled herself to learn the Efik language, regarding it as unchristian and undesirable).

Once I have arrived at my destination I shall write again but it may be some time before the next letter reaches you. Please look in upon my mother.

Your true friend
Mary

CHAPTER SIX

Mary's canoe paddled gently up to the riverbank and the oarsmen called for assistance from the people standing silently watching. She had been told there might be a welcome party. Mary had become well known beyond her original territory. Word had spread of her unusual style and friendly attitude.

Once up river Mary felt strangely more at home than in Duke Town. Villagers stood shyly on the banks as the canoes were guided in. Their smiles were broad and Mary called to them in Efik. Their smiles grew wider and two small boys leapt into the water to help carry her belongings. Women and children huddled together watching and pointing as Mary clambered out, helped again by the two boys. Mary laughed softly to herself, clearly her hair and skin colour were a major attraction. They must have heard about her already: practically the whole village had come to see the famous white woman with the burning hair who taught 'book' and spoke in words that all could understand. Mary was delighted to find such a warm welcome. She was sure that this was going to be a success. The crowd parted to make way for someone very important. 'Welcome to our village Ma Slessor. I am Chief Edem.

We met once at the big palaver. You have changed a little in two years. The moon is less about your skin as once it was. Will you come to eat and talk? ' he said indicating a large hut a short distance away.

'Thank you for your hospitality Chief Edem. I do remember you. I had heard you were a generous man. I am honoured by your kindness.' The chief laughed and nodded.

'Indeed you are most welcome. We have heard much of your skills in teaching 'book' and your wisdom amongst the foolish.' Mary laughed quietly - perhaps the chief had met Mrs. Henshaw! 'Let's have a palaver and forget the foolish, for today we celebrate a new beginning.'

They settled down to a feast of beans, rice, yams and fish. It had been a long journey but Mary felt only excitement, as the future looked very promising. Chief Edem provided Mary with a plot of land near his compound so that she could build a mission house.

Mary soon became well liked and respected by many people, and her bible lessons were well attended. Many villagers were keen to have the children taught the 'book' and Mary spent many happy months with her large class.

One day however, Mary discovered that a woman was to be punished for breaking the law of the village. The punishment was a terrible one. The frightened woman was surrounded by a crowd of villagers. A man was walking slowly towards her swinging a ladle of boiling oil. His job was to pour the oil over the trapped woman as her punishment. Mary realized that it was not so different from her days in Dundee when a lump of lead was swinging towards her. She knew she had to act fast. Swallowing her nerves she looked the man in the eye and walked slowly between him and the terrified woman. The man with the ladle wasn't sure what to do. Eventually he turned to face his chief and put the ladle to one side.

Edem had been watching from the shade of his hut. He slowly stood up and clapped his hands twice. Immediately two of his slaves knelt before him and he spoke to them briefly. They bowed and then told Mary that she could have the woman if she wished. Edem smiled as Mary thanked him for his mercy. He walked away, no longer interested in the situation.

The crowd whispered that this white woman must

have great power. The woman was untied and helped into Mary's hut. Only afterwards did Mary stop to consider what might have happened.

Gradually, Mary and Chief Edem grew to like and respect one another. He admired her courage and she admired his willingness to accept new ideas. Time passed and the letters continued. Sometimes the news from home was worrying.

1883
Old Town

Dearest Mother
I am sorry to hear you are both so frail. Please bid my darling sister rest and do the same yourself. I am vexed to hear of you both in such distress. I pray God will comfort you while I cannot. The good news is that my second furlough approaches and I will soon be home to tend you both. I have great news and a wonderful surprise to make you smile. The urge to tell is great but I shall hold my peace and let you discover it soon.
As always
With fondest love
Mary

1883
Old Town

Dear Elspeth
My warmest thanks for your attendance upon my mother and sister. [Sosono as they say round here!] In their last letter they sang the praises of your broth and clootie dumpling. Even

the tiniest morsel is a benefit. Speaking of tiny morsels, I have some good news! When I next come home I shall not be alone. I shall be bringing my sweet wee baby! [I have named her after my youngest sister Janie – do you remember her?] This beautiful child, a gift from God, came to me in the most horrid circumstances. It is the custom in these parts to regard twins as cursed. For many years twins were killed or abandoned in the jungle, their mother banished for ever. Three months ago there was a great cry in the village. A local woman had given birth to twins and was forced to leave her home, family and friends. One of the children in my reading school came running to tell me so I flew to the hut where she lay weeping as they threw her belongings about. The crowd had already caused the death of one infant during the chaos but I managed to rescue the other. There was much anger,noise and disagreement but, after a palaver, I managed to persuade the chief that if he allowed the woman to stay I would look after the child and any curse would of course fall upon me and not upon the village.

Thankfully the villagers were happy with this suggestion and the babe was saved. She is truly beautiful with eyes the colour of walnuts. I shall become a mother to all twins until I can persuade these people that there is no curse.

This task is great for the villagers are very fearful of curses and the Juju, dark magic as they call it. They see signs in everyday things and have countless customs. Many times I have seen an honest man, woman or child harshly treated. Only last week two silly girls crept into the boys' yard after dark and were caught so doing. In these parts that is a terrible crime and they were sentenced to a hundred lashes. Had this been allowed those girls would have died long before the hundredth stroke. They were children playing a foolish prank yet it was one which nearly cost their lives. With much palaver I persuaded the Chief to show mercy and they were given ten lashes. Their backs are badly cut and will take many weeks to heal but at least they are alive.

Goodness gracious I have written a great deal more than I intended. Please do not tell my mother or sister of my news, I want it to be a surprise. What news do you have from home?

Your tale of the runaway pig at the market had me roaring with laughter. We had a similar problem a few weeks ago when one of the goats ran amok through the crops. Most of the children from the school ran after it but the goat was much faster and wilier. The children thought it great fun but the women did not. It trampled many of the new baskets and had it not been needed for milk, it may have ended up as goat stew!

Anyway, I have more letters to write to the district commissioner. Many people seem to be travelling to visit me with tales of problems with their masters or their land. Their faith in me is flattering but I hope not unfounded. They see me as their voice among the white men and I shall speak for them whenever I can. So, after this long epistle I shall bid you farewell until my next furlough in three months time. [Janie will be six months old by then and twice as pretty as she is now.]

Your faithful friend

Mary

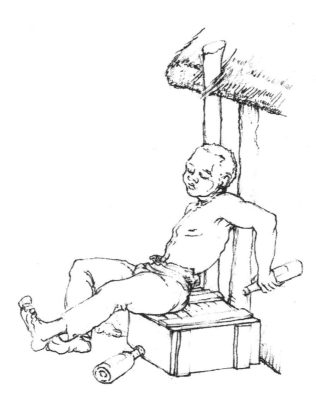

CHAPTER SEVEN

Much of Mary's time was spent in sorting out troubles between tribes and trying to change drinking habits. The traders brought gin and rum up the river, but not enough milk for the children. Mary believed that most troubles came about because of the rum and gin drunk so frequently. She was clever and used local customs to avoid troubles starting, but it was hard work.

One night as she sat weaving, the lamp sputtered and she knew that it needed more oil. She laid her weaving down and rubbed her head. She had not realised the time. Her baby had been asleep for hours now and would soon awaken for a feed. The cans of milk were precious and Mary worried that they would not last; if so how long could she feed her baby? She chewed her lip as she wondered how long the fighting to the east would continue. Supplies would be hard to get if rival warriors were blocking the routes or lying in wait for unsuspecting traders. Mary cursed the gin and the rum brought by the traders. It made the young men irritable and trigger happy. Violence was all around and Mary longed for an end to it.

There was so much beauty and joy in Calabar. The fighting and drunkenness was so unnecessary. This was a region rich in food and resources. Already the villagers were starting to heed Mary's suggestions that trade and barter might be better than rum and fighting. Mary had spoken with the chief about rubber, mango and basket trading. She was hopeful that this might be the way forward. Since her arrival the village had become more prosperous and copper rods were piling up around them. The rods were made in the larger townships and were used instead of money. Mary had found the system strange to begin with, but now she gave it little thought. All she cared about was getting enough to care for her children.

She paused for a moment and wondered how many rods would pay for another two rooms on her mission house. Many more women and children were finding their way to Mary's mission house and she turned no-one away. Her growing family of adopted twins was a source of both joy and worry to her.

There simply wasn't the space for all the bodies occupying it. She spent most of her time trying to teach or nurse in very difficult situations. Little did Mary know there would be more difficulties in the months and years ahead.

CHAPTER EIGHT

Old Town

January 1886

My dear Elspeth

It grieves me sorely to write this letter but I must do so or I shall crumble. To lose my mother in this way seems a harsh trial but I cling to the thought that her suffering is over. Her health had been failing for some time and yet, it still feels strange to think of her gone. I rock my children to sleep and sing 'Bee baw babbity' to them as she did for me. I'm glad mother got to know Janie so well before she died. They loved each other so. That last visit home on furlough was full of laughter. Mother really seemed a little better when Janie was there.

Janie is toddling around as I write but my two bonny boys lie asleep in the corner. The house is getting more crowded by the day – I hear another two sets of twins will arrive soon from a village three days trek from here. I would have walked to fetch them myself but my legs are still weakened from that last bout of sickness. There have been many deaths from disease and I pray that the children will be spared.

When I am stronger I shall teach the older children to gather the medicinal herbs we are growing in our compound. They are already helping to do the chores. Their happy faces help me in my dark moments when grief grips me.

Finally I must thank you for the Christmas pudding you sent. It was sent to surrounding villages and the bowl it came in was a great prize and much admired. I have it on my shelf and it will prove very useful in the months to come with so many mouths to feed.

The mission house needs at least two more rooms and I am considering building another storey. With many hands it should be done before the rainy season begins in April. I shall write again soon. In the meantime please write some foolish nonsense to cheer me

Your friend
Mary.

Mary was just sealing the envelope on this letter when she heard a terrible cry from outside. 'Ma Slessor! Ma Slessor! Come quick. A terrible thing's happened!'

Mary dropped the letter and hurried to the door. Janie was crying and pointing in the direction of the chief's hut. She was too upset to speak so she hurried on. Many villagers were rushing towards the clearing behind the

chief's compound. Mary followed them and realised
something was indeed terribly wrong. Women were wailing
and the chief was crouching over something on the ground,
surrounded by some of his men. Mary walked over to the
chief and stood behind him. His men leaned forward and
then she saw. The chief's son, Etim, lay groaning on the
ground, unmoving. A large log lay beside him.

'What happened?' whispered Mary softly.
'He was cutting down wood to build a new hut.' replied
the chief staring bleakly at his son. With a nod of the head
his men lifted Etim gently from the ground and started to
carry him to the chief's hut. Each step made Etim gasp.
The log had struck him on the neck and he could not move.
His neck was broken.

Edem's wives and slaves nursed Etim for several days but there was little change so the chief sent for the witch doctor. He arrived swiftly and made a grand entrance. His face bore streaks of grey powdery ash and his eyes were wild. He danced around Etim shrieking and muttering. He tossed a small leather pouch into the air and let its contents tumble to floor. Bones, stones, herbs and gems scattered on the dust floor of the hut.

'Betrayal! Wickedness! Juju! Someone has cast an evil spell upon your family.' He declared, turning to the chief. There was a gasp from the women attending Etim and the witch doctor twisted round and pointed to one.

'This one here is responsible.' He said, pointing to a horrified attendant who shook her head furiously but was too shocked to speak. The chief glared at her and ordered everyone away from his son.

'Make my son well,' he begged the witch doctor, his eyes wet with tears. The witch doctor nodded and then continued his dance around Etim. He ordered fires to be lit, and herbs to be gathered. He tried all his best spells. He blew smoke into Etim's nose and mouth. He shouted in Etim's ear to drive out any demons. But on the fourth day Etim died.

The chief could not contain his sorrow. He demanded that the woman who had been accused be brought before him, to stand trial according to the old laws. Mary ran from her hut to plead with him. She knew that the method for trial was poison bean. It had to be taken as a drink made from crushed beans. Anyone suspected of witchcraft would be expected to drink it. If the person survived, they were considered guilty, and would be put to death. If they did not survive, they were considered innocent. So the accused person couldn't win.

Mary knew the poison was very strong and that few people had ever survived. This was her most difficult challenge so far. She thought back to her days in Dundee facing bullying schoolmates and angry gangs. She thought of the times she had saved the twins. She thought about the hundred lashes. Her sharp tongue and quick wit had helped her many a time. She hoped that she could succeed this time too but she was not sure it was possible. The only thing she was sure of was that she must try.

Chief Edem was sitting outside his hut. Villagers kept at a respectful distance and voices were hushed. No-one wished to anger or disturb him. A word from the witch doctor could mean certain death for any of them. The whole village had gathered for the trial. People began to sit quietly in a semi circle, facing the chief. The accused woman was sitting between two guards, shaking and weeping. Chief Edem was stony-faced, his eyes fixed on the body of his son. Etim lay on a rushmat, wrapped loosely in blanket. A slave timidly waved a palm frond above his body to keep the flies away.

Chief Edem gave a long sigh and wearily looked at the accused woman.

'Why did you cast a spell for misfortune on my house?' he demanded.

'I swear I have done nothing!' cried the woman, frantically searching the crowd for assistance. Few would meet her desperate eyes.

'Prove yourself then by taking the poison bean trial. Drink the esere bean.' said the chief, rising from his seat. The woman sobbed, sank to her knees and shook her head. The witch doctor's eyes glittered as he approached with

the potion.

Everyone feared the gourd and its terrible contents. Mary stepped forward. There was a shocked silence as she approached the chief. Surely she was going too far this time?

'Chief Edem, I too have known grief and my heart is sorrowed for the loss of your son. You have always been a wise and merciful man. Etim was taken from you by accident, this woman is not to blame. There has been no spell.' Her words were soft and soothing. The chief angrily turned his back on her.

'This does not concern you Ma Slessor. I must have justice for my son. The old ways are needed now – go home to your reading school.'

Mary thought for a moment before saying, 'I shall go home, Chief Edem, if you give me your word you will not act this day, but sleep on it.' Chief Edem's shoulders rose and fell as a huge sigh escaped his body.

'This is not your place to speak Ma Slessor. I am chief of the Ekenge people. My people look to me for the law. You have been made welcome in our village, but this is not your concern.'

'Great chief, many times we have had a palaver. Your wisdom is known in Ekenge and far across Okoyong territory. But your heart is heavy, and you should rest before you set your mind to the law. A wise man such as you does not rush to act.'

'I will not rush Ma Slessor but some things cannot wait. Juju will come if my son is not avenged and lies upon the earth another day.' He said quietly, glancing at his son's body.

'The time is near to bury your son my friend but sleep another night before you act, I beg you. If you have ever trusted me before, trust me now in this. Your son deserves the best that we can give.'

'Very well, we shall make a big palaver tomorrow but the old ways will be done.'

Mary thanked him quickly and left. She knew that the woman was safe at least for one more day. She was tied to a stake but she was alive. And while she was alive

there was hope.

Early the next day Mary went to visit the chief. She invited him to walk and talk with her. She argued that the poison bean trial would not take away his pain.

'You do not understand Ma. My son needs to be buried and this I cannot do without ceremony and sacrifice. The old ways demand it.'

Mary listened carefully and then had an idea. She discussed it with the chief, who was exhausted by his ordeal, and knew in his heart that Mary's words made sense. Inside, Mary's heart rejoiced – the woman was saved! She set to work immediately for there was much to be done.

Etim's body was dressed in fine clothes from Mary's
mission box and sat upon a makeshift throne. His body
was surrounded by skulls, herbs, gems, fruit and flowers.
This was to indicate his importance as son of a chief.
Villagers came from miles around to see the sight and Chief

Etim was pleased. It was a strangely grand scene yet it satisfied the chief and the accused woman was allowed to go free. A cow was sacrificed and placed with the body in the burial plot later that day. For many centuries it had been the custom to have a human sacrifice so this was a great improvement. Mary's skill at finding the right answer to difficult situations had led her to be regarded as a wise and trustworthy person.

CHAPTER NINE

Mary spent many happy years in Calabar. She loved the place and its peoples. As she grew old in their midst, she kept her sense of fun. One day she was given a bicycle as a gift. This was a most welcome addition to her meagre belongings. For almost forty years, Mary had walked hundreds of miles across Calabar; west through Okoyong and Ibibio, even as far north as Ibo, nursing the sick, teaching and settling disputes. The bike would help her reach people faster. She was delighted!

As she rode about the dusty roads on it villagers laughed at this strange sight. Her old, skinny legs stuck out like gnarled old branches as she pedalled. Everyone called the bicycle '*Enan Ukwak*' – 'the iron cow'. Wherever Mary rode, a crowd of squealing children would follow. At first only the bravest of the brave would dare try to ride the iron cow. Eventually though Mary's family and friends were arguing about turns to ride it.

Many times Mary was asked to sort out disputes. She became so good at it that she was asked to be in charge of the most senior court in the land. Sometimes she dealt with things very quickly and in her own way. She even hit people over the head with her umbrella if she was angry with them. Everyone agreed that she was always fair so no-one ever complained about her unusual way of resolving problems. She was loved and trusted by hundreds of people. Over the years she helped create many schools and hospitals for people in Calabar and beyond. Eventually, she became known as *Eka Kpukpro Owo* – the mother of all peoples.

During her time in Africa, Mary had battled against malaria. Sometimes she had been so ill that she had been sent home to Scotland to recover; but she always came back to her beloved Calabar. Each time she fell ill, her body became a little weaker though she was a determined fighter. She even joked about her health; 'poor hair! Poor head! It is as bald as a sixpence all over the back…The few hairs left at the front are like those of a doll's head put on with bad glue.'

But her many years of hard work, illness and poor diet had taken their toll.

Over Christmas 1914, while working in the village of Use,

Mary's health took a turn for the worse. She collapsed, and was unable to walk; so she told her family to carry her to church services. They wanted her to rest - but Mary had been stubborn all her days, and she wasn't about to change now.

Mary planned to make one last journey to Scotland; but sadly it was not to be. On January 13th 1915 Mary became very ill once more. Her friends and family gathered around her and listened as she prayed in Efik.

'Abasi, sana mi yak.' ['O God, release me.']

She died peacefully shortly after.

When news of her death spread across the country there was great sorrow. Hundreds of people lined the road to the cemetery. Flags flew at half-mast. Tributes came from all over. She was much loved and sorely missed. Her children and friends continued the work she began, in memory of her.

Today in Use, a small cairn by the roadside marks the place where she died. On a hillside above Duke Town there is a huge granite cross sent from Aberdeen as a memorial. North-east of Use, is the Mary Slessor Mission Hospital at Itu.

Mary left a tremendous legacy in the area. To this day she is fondly remembered in Calabar, and throughout Nigeria. Interestingly, she is less well-known in her homeland, although there are some places to visit in Dundee. Her face can also be seen on some Scottish banknotes. None of this would have interested Mary though. She hated fuss and was very modest. When people acknowledged her achievements she described it as 'blarney'. She scoffed at any publicity. The attention baffled and amused her. However, determination and a big heart were Mary's trademark – something even she could not deny. Shortly before she died Mary wrote to a friend, 'I'm a wee, wee wifie, very little buikit [built] - but I grip on well nonetheless!'

GLOSSARY

A'BODY everybody

BIRL spin

CA'ED ME O'ER   knocked me over

CHAPPIN' knocking

CLOOTIE DUMPLING   steamed pudding

COUP tip

CRY call

DICHT wipe

DONNERT stupid

DREICH   dismal, grey, overcast

FEART afraid

GAFFER   supervisor, boss

GETTIN' YOUR BOOKS   being sacked

GEY very

HAUD hold

HIRPLIN' hobbling

KEN know

MIDDEN place to dump rubbish

PALAVER talk

QUINE female

SPEUG sparrow

VEX worry

Reader's Notes

This story is a fictional account of some of the major events in the life of Mary Slessor. The characters of Elspeth, Mrs Henshaw and Katie Murray are fictional. The sequence of events has been altered somewhat for the purposes of the story.

Calabar is now known as Nigeria and during the 1800s was subject to almost constant tribal unrest. Unofficially, a posting to the area was considered a death sentence whether through disease or tribal attack.

This story is not a biography but a tribute to the work and life of Mary Slessor who did much to alleviate the suffering of others and promote positive social change. Mary worked hard to combat prejudice and injustice wherever she could. Much of the prejudice came from her own contemporaries within the missionary community. They found her unorthodox approach difficult to accept. This was, however, short-lived as her successes grew.

Mary was a pioneer of equality and recognised the value of communication. Her respect for local people and disregard of convention allowed her to make incredible progress. Despite initially facing significant barriers and open hostility, Mary earned the respect of the local inhabitants and those of people far beyond Calabar.

Teachers reading this may wish to note that this book dovetails with the Scottish curriculum in

- Environmental Studies
- Personal and Social Health Education
- Philosophy
- Language

Further information on Rooshie-Doo books, and suggestions for their use in schools, can be found on the publisher's website at www.galluspublications.com

If you have enjoyed this book, you may also enjoy…

Reformed! A story of Jenny Geddes by Helen Welsh

Murderers! A story of Burke and Hare by Karen Doherty

Accused! A story of Beatrix Laing by Susan Greig

Cannibals! A story of Sawney Bean by Helen Welsh